BEANBOY

by GEORGE SHANNON
pictures by PETER SIS

GREENWILLOW BOOKS
NEW YORK

To my brothers—John, Stuart, and Arthur—G.S.   To my father—P.S.

Text copyright © 1984 by George W. B. Shannon
Illustrations copyright © 1984 by Peter Sis
All rights reserved. No part of this book
may be reproduced or utilized in any form
or by any means, electronic or mechanical,
including photocopying, recording or by
any information storage and retrieval
system, without permission in writing
from the Publisher, Greenwillow Books,
a division of William Morrow & Company, Inc.,
105 Madison Avenue, New York, N.Y. 10016.
Printed in the United States of America
First Edition
10 9 8 7 6 5 4 3 2 1

Library of Congress Cataloging in Publication Data
Shannon, George.   Bean boy.
Summary: An orphan with only a tin cup full of beans learns
to survive with the help and advice of kindly people he meets.
[1. Orphans—Fiction] I. Sis, Peter, ill. II. Title.
PZ7.S5287Be 1984   [E]   83-20764
ISBN 0-688-03779-8   ISBN 0-688-03780-1 (lib. bdg.)

There once was a boy who lived all alone. No father, no mother, no sister, no brother. Not even a pet. All he had were the clothes he wore and an old tin cup filled up with beans.

To make the beans last as long as could be, he only ate one each day for lunch and saved the rest for later. But later soon came, and one morning when he looked in his cup, there was only one bean left.

When I eat that bean, he told himself, I'll have nothing left but the cup, and I can't eat the cup. It's time for me to find a job.

So off he went, down the road with his very last bean jangling at the bottom of his old tin cup. The boy looked and looked, but no matter where he went there were no jobs. He walked until the moon and the cold had both come out, and he was tired and hungry.

4

He stopped at a house and knocked on the door.

"Please," he asked, "do you have a place I could sleep tonight and some food to share? I'm all by myself. No father, no mother, no sister, no brother. All I have in all the world is this old tin cup with one bean inside."

"Yes," said the man. "Come in. Come in. There's plenty of stew and you can sleep by the fire."

The boy said thanks and was soon asleep. Now as he slept, he turned and rolled, and when he rolled, his hand tipped the cup and the bean rolled out across the floor.

And before he had even snored once more, a rat ran up and began to crunch and chew up the bean.

The noise woke the boy, who began to cry so loud he woke up the man. "Now what am I supposed to do? All I had in the whole wide world was that one last bean and now your rat went and ate my bean."

The man felt sorry, and as he didn't want rats in his house anyway, he said, "Since it ate your bean, it seems only right that you take the rat."

So off went the boy with his old tin cup and the bean-eating rat on the end of a string.

Once again, he looked for a job, but there was none to be found. Soon night came around again and the boy hadn't had one bite to eat.

Cold and tired, he stopped at a house.

"Please, do you have a place I could sleep tonight and some food to share? I'm all by myself. No father, no mother, no sister, no brother. All I have in all the world is this old tin cup and this rat that ate my very last bean."

"Come in," said the woman. "There's cheese and bread that you can have and a pillow in the corner where you can sleep."

The boy said thanks and was soon asleep with the cup in one hand and the string that led to the rat in the other. He slept so soundly he didn't hear the cat walk by. But the cat saw the rat and swallowed it down in one single gulp!

When the boy woke up the next morning, he pulled on his string, but instead of a rat, a smiling cat was at the other end.

"Now what am I supposed to do?" cried the boy. "All I had in the whole wide world was my old tin cup and the rat that ate my very last bean. And now your cat went and ate my rat."

The woman was so eager for the boy to hush up she said, "Since my cat ate your rat, it seems only right that you take the cat. Goodbye."

So off went the boy with his old tin cup and the rat-eating cat on the end of a string. He looked and looked for a job again, but there was none to be found. Night came again and he hadn't had a bite to eat all day.

Once again he stopped at a house. "Please," he said, "do you have a place I could sleep tonight and some food to share? I'm all by myself. No father, no mother, no sister, no brother. All I have in all the world is this old tin cup and this cat that ate the rat that ate my very last bean."

"Yes," said the baker. "You can sleep in the chair and I've got some raisins and nuts you can have."

The boy said thanks and was soon asleep with the cup in one hand and the string that led to the cat in the other. Everything could have been fine that night if the dog hadn't crept in and scared off the cat.

The screams of the cat woke up the boy, but all he could find was a grinning dog.

"Now what am I supposed to do?" cried the boy so loud he woke up the baker. "All I had in the whole wide world was my old tin cup and the cat that ate the rat that ate my very last bean. And now your dog has scared away my cat."

"Well," said the baker, feeling sad for the boy, "since my dog scared away your cat, it seems only right that you take the dog."

So off the boy went with his old tin cup and the cat-scaring dog on the end of a string. He looked again all day that day, but could not find a job.

Once more it was night and the boy hadn't eaten a single bite. He stopped at a blacksmith's and asked as before.

"Please, do you have a place I could sleep tonight and some food to share? I'm all by myself. No father, no mother, no sister, no brother. All I have in all the world is this old tin cup and this dog that scared the cat that ate the rat that ate my very last bean."

"Sure enough," said the blacksmith. "You can sleep in the barn. There's plenty of straw and you can have some gravy and the biscuit crumbs."

The boy said thanks and was soon asleep in a pile of straw with his cup in one hand and the string that led to the dog in the other. Though the boy slept soundly, the donkey nearby had a terrible dream that made him kick. And when he kicked, he kicked the dog clear out of the barn and off through the sky too far to see.

"Now what am I supposed to do?" cried the boy as he woke up to see his dog sailing off toward the moon. "All I had in the whole wide world was my old tin cup and the dog that scared the cat that ate the rat that ate the very last bean I had. And now your donkey has kicked away my dog."

"Well," said the blacksmith, afraid of what the neighbors would think, "since my donkey kicked away your dog, it seems only right that you take the donkey."

So off the boy went with his old tin cup and the dog-kicking donkey on the end of a string. He looked all day, but found no job. And the only place to stop that night was a small farmhouse.

"Please," he said, "do you have a place I could sleep tonight and some food to share? I'm all by myself. No father, no mother, no sister, no brother. All I have in all the world is this old tin cup and this donkey that kicked the dog that scared the cat that ate the rat that ate the very last bean I had."

"Well," said the farmer, "I don't have much room, but I've got lots of beans. Give me your cup and I'll fill it up."

The boy said, "Thanks. I'll only eat one bean a day to make them last as long as I can."

"No need to do that," said the farmer. And he told the boy of a much better way to make his beans last.

So when the boy set off the next morning, he didn't need to look for a job. He went back home and planted half his cup of beans.

By the time he'd eaten the other half, he'd grown enough for twenty cups.

And on and on, until that boy had beans to eat and plant and sell, and still more left to share with friends.